OILY SKIES OF FIRE

BRIAN D. HINSON

Published by Water Dragon Publishing
waterdragonpublishing.com

Experience our other Dragon Gems titles
waterdragonpublishing.com/dragon-gems

ISBN 978-1-969655-00-5 (Trade Paperback)

FIRST EDITION

10 9 8 7 6 5 4 3 2 1

OILY SKIES OF FIRE

4 NOVEMBER 1916

A PURPLE PRE-DAWN with cold, still air greeted me on this day of glory. Or the day of my death, depending on how things shook out in the next few hours. This had kept my eyes open throughout the night, despite a little Kirschwasser before bed. Emil leaned in and whispered, "It's not too late to force a puke and leave this to the backup squad."

"And allow someone else the glory?" My breath plumed ghosts in the dim pre-dawn as my false smile faltered and I adjusted my leather helmet for the eleventh time.

Emil removed his peaked officer hat to run a hand through his dishwater blond hair. We both had our habits when stressed. He placed the stepladder in the frosted grass beside my red Fokker triplane. I stuck out my gloved hand and he surprised me with a hug, which I returned with equal ferocity. Once broken, he adjusted my woolen scarf as I glanced around, wary of crew seeing the display. Silly, I know. Why shouldn't there be a hug before a risky, first-of-its-kind mission?

"Lieutenant Johann Fischer, good luck," said Emil formally as he saluted.

"Thank you, Lieutenant Emil Hahn. We shall meet again in two hours!" I returned the salute.

I climbed into the cockpit just above the second wing of the three. I slipped on my goggles as Emil moved the ladder to the rear and then positioned himself by the prop. I switched the magneto on and pushed the throttle to full. I signaled Emil with an upturned thumb. He shoved the prop downward and the engine roared to life. I throttled back to idle and kept my feet on the brakes.

Unfortunately, these flying machines were not quiet.

After a final wave to Emil I taxied on this thin strip hewn from the Black Forest, the edges lit by lanterns spaced at forty-foot intervals. A fully cleared circle would serve better for unpredictable winds upon landing and take-off, but secrecy was paramount.

I turned the Fokker in a hairpin fashion to face the full length of the strip. A white spotlight halfway up, where I had started, signaled with two short flashes. That meant Lieutenant Schneider, my counterpart for the mission, had started his plane successfully.

I pushed the throttle to full and rolled ahead through the still, cold air. Perfect for a flight. Less than perfect for the enemy. The lanterns rushed by as I accelerated beyond the point where the forces of lift exceeded the weight of my fully-fueled aircraft, and the ground dropped away. A smile grew, despite my nerves. The exhilaration of flight never disappointed.

Forty-five minutes into the flight we neared Feldberg Mountain, the peak laden with a late Autumn snow. I pulled back on the throttle and dropped altitude from 8,000 feet, the engine quieting as its labors diminished. Schneider maintained level flight behind, and now above me.

The peak stood about 5,000 feet above sea level. I executed a gentle descending spiral, the crest at the center. Anxiety prickled my skin to gooseflesh. Gusty winds about the peak buffeted me as I dipped below 6,000 feet. They had to have heard the droning of the aircraft. It would be a disappointment, and yet, a relief, if no one emerged to check the noisy machine descending. But no glory. My chances of survival were much greater without tempting glory.

There. My breath caught. Off to my left and below, black, as the professors had predicted, stark against the snow, the wingspan twice longer than mine. The head bore two horns, a female then, and turned to fix her gaze at me, her serpentine neck positioned in a question mark. I wished she had the equivalent feeling of my own raised hair. But I doubted it. She was merely curious at this juncture.

In my rising anxiety (and, I loathe to admit, fear) I nearly forgot the second phase of the mission: photography. I plucked the Goertz camera from my flight bag and steadied it with one hand, bracing against the edge of the cockpit, propwash doing its best to send the camera to a certain death thousands of feet below. I snapped one, levered to advance the film, snapped another. The first photographs of a dragon in flight by a man in flight! The camera dropped back into the bag as I looked behind for Schneider, who maintained his position above. Now phase three would begin: Lead the beast with fire in her belly away from Schneider.

I kept descending, but added throttle. More noise would make her more curious, at least that was the argument. Yes, she followed, her great wings beating in an effort for a closer look. By all accounts, untested accounts, the Fokker was faster. Dragons were gliders. My hands gripped *powered* flight. One hundred and fifteen horses spun my propeller, and I throttled every single horse now. I leveled out for the race. The maximum range of the fiery breath was estimated to be 100 yards. Plenty of distance presently. She thrashed her wings as my Fokker outpaced her, but not my much.

Despite the cold, I sweat. Looking back, I spied Schneider bearing down on her from above, closing with the black hibernation guard. She appeared unaware, intent only on me, as Schneider dived with his engine idle.

I kept looking behind, the dragon keeping pace. I couldn't hear the staccato thrum of Schneider's 7.92-millimeter dual machine guns, but the light of his gunfire strobed in tracer streaks. The dragon bellowed, the roar shaking my bones despite the heavy drone of my engine. She'd been hit! I raised my fist and cheered. Blood sprayed behind her as a pink mist. Her head turned as her toothy maw, large enough to take the tail from my aircraft, dripped saliva to the winds. She folded her wings, twisted and dove in a manner so nimble as to defy belief. The blows Schneider had dealt were not fatal.

I turned, adding full right rudder, tilting the wings to the edge of stall and the loss of lift. If I maneuvered below stall speed in my steep turn, I would drop almost like a brick.

He attempted a climb at full throttle. But she closed the distance far too fast. She spewed potassium chlorate and a reactive sucrose from different orifices in the roof of her mouth which combined to produce a yellow flame that engulfed Schneider's Fokker. The wood and fabric of the wings and fuselage had no chance against a direct hit of intense, liquid fire. I stopped breathing as I watched his aircraft disintegrate into flaming debris trailed by black smoke against the cold, blue sky.

I was still in the midst of my turn. I pulled back on the stick and fired my own guns at her as I continued through my turn to flee. If I chased without scoring a fatal shot, she would be able to execute her snap turn and be upon me, and the mission, and my life, forfeit. I had no way to ascertain if her two fire sacs had more fuel, but I couldn't take that chance. I turned south toward the base, that thin landing strip in the Black Forest. Where I had to report Schneider's death.

And my retreat.

•   •   •

That evening, after the longest debrief of my career, Emil and I sat in Lörrach's tavern, snifters of Kirschwasser before us. The wooden russet roof beams and floor had stood for two centuries but the electric sconces along the walls burned with the cold light of a new, changed, and technological world. I missed the warmth and comfort of gas lanterns and candles.

The excitement of the day had given me an abundance of anxious energy. I doubted sleep would come tonight. The brandy might help.

My eyes caught Emil staring. He moved his hand forward to brush mine for the smallest of moments. A slight, insignificant touch, but with coded meaning. In public, this was the strongest signal of affection we dared. Damn the Roman religion of this continent and its senseless sexual "mores." In the Americas, their religions dictated nothing so cruel. So advanced their nations, my eyes greened like spring with envy. It was Lolar brothers of the Wabanaki Confederacy that had invented powered flight, twelve years past. Brilliant men who had made bicycles before their world-transforming discovery.

"Pity you didn't kill her," said Emil said softly, running his hand through his gelled dishwater blonde hair. A charming habit.

"Pity she killed Schneider."

We raised or glasses and said together, "Rest in peace, dear Harri Schneider."

We drank. I had drained my remaining Kirschwasser. My part in the mission, the decoy, had been deemed the higher risk. Yet it had been Schneider who died in an immolation of fire.

"What do you think they will do, now?" asked Emil, staring into his snifter and its clear liquid. "I mean, *really*? I know the calculations of the generals."

"I agree with their assessment. They cannot strike until the spring, when the cold-blooded snakes can fly and fight with all their power. I say bring in the artillery, guarded with a whole damn fleet of aeroplanes, and bring Feldberg Mountain down atop them."

"Bold. But Feldberg wouldn't crumble. And no man would dare enter their warrens." Emil drained the remainder of his brandy. "No duty tomorrow, right?"

I nodded. "I need the rest."

"I can think of a better way to spend the day."

I snorted. Anyone overhearing would think he spoke of whores, a common pursuit of military men. But spending the time as Emil proposed certainly charmed. "You have leave?"

"I do."

"You bring this up now?"

"I wanted it as a surprise after your mission. If you managed to survive." His gallows humor always delighted me, despite the dark undercurrents.

No use in drinking conservatively this night. "The cabin?"

Emil nodded and smiled. Wasn't this a perfect storm? I survived a fight with a dragon—yet, should we? Schneider's death tugged at my soul. A traditional man's man, if you will, brave to a fault. Would a night (and day) of joyous forbidden sexual celebration be out of order? Would we do him dishonor? He was a comrade-in-arms and I had witnessed his death. The grim scene kept turning over and over in my mind.

"You know," began Emil, once again peering into my thoughts, "if we did go out whoring, Schneider would be honored. You know he would. His ghost might ask that we shout his name at the climax."

I laughed. Too loudly for not yet being properly inebriated so I stifled my cackle with a hand. Emil was right. The man had several crosses and an icon of the Virgin Mary in his cockpit and it was the gay pilot that survived. "Well, then, let's do him the honor, then. In our own way."

•　　　•　　　•

Dearest Elsabeth,

I apologize for the infrequency of my letters, but the work has been intense and unrelenting. I can say no more, military secrecy and all. But I want you to know that I am safe and in no danger. You worry much and I do too little to assuage your fears.

I know this may sound odd, but pray for a cold winter. My stipend should keep you and little Wilhelm stocked in coal. Please keep me apprised of his boyish exploits. They warm my heart so.

With Love and Hope,
Johann

•   •   •

24 NOVEMBER 1916

Unseasonable, humid, and dangerous came a warm spell. We had struck the hornet's nest while it lay dormant, and dallied in the decision-making to follow. We all thought we had more time. And it turned out Schneider did kill the guard dragon, her body discovered by hunters. Her wounds had been survivable for less than an hour. Good for him and his epitaph.

Two hundred Fokkers had rolled off the assembly lines this year, yet we had only one hundred twenty qualified pilots. The planes could only fly for two hours before refueling. The dragons could glide aloft for a full day. Hidden airstrips dotted the Black Forest, and it was determined that we keep squadrons fueled and ready for the coming attack. Reconnaissance flights circled on the regular. The dragons didn't know the location of our bases, so it was believed they would strike nearby cities in their thirst for vengeance.

I worried for Elsabeth and Wilhelm, north in Stuttgart.

Emil rotated in the scheduled reconnaissance flights. They remained aloft for an hour and a half until my squadron of twelve launched.

As I gloomily expected, half an hour into our flight as the sun arced from the horizon bringing the last gasp of summer, the dragons were spotted emerging from the Feldberg nests. The telephone contact notified our base, and our airborne captain jotted down the morse code message from the strobing light: seventeen dragons headed toward Kirchzarten. We followed the captain, wagging his wings, in formation to intercept.

The captain's calculations took us on a northeast vector, seven thousand feet. The winged reptiles would hear us before we spotted them, this was assured. We hoped to still have the higher altitude advantage before they rushed to meet this new technological threat from humanity. As my stopwatch indicated that we'd reached the possible vicinity of the enemy, I scanned the clear skies with my binoculars.

As per military flight instructions, when I sighted them below and turning up to meet us, I tilted my wings to and fro with vigor and vectored a descending turn to meet the threat. By the time everyone got the signal, we were no longer in a tight V formation, but scattered in a lopsided W. And the dragons favored their inverted V, a commendable strategy to encircle their less dexterous enemies.

Our double-barrel machine guns far outstripped their fiery breath in range, and made up for the deficit in maneuverability. The sky streaked with yellow lines of magnesium-tipped lead seeking scaley targets. My teeth clenched hard enough to crack enamel, but no matter. I stared down the gaping gullets that would soon spit fire as I sat in the midst of three wings fashioned of a flammable fabric.

I knew Emil's squadron had lifted in support, but would they arrive before our more numerous and nimbler foe immolated us all? And after our threat was neutralized, the town of Kirchzarten? Hopefully the citizens had enough warning to retreat underground to weather the coming firestorm.

One, then two, then by the gods of the Americas, three dragons dropped flailing from formation! Their wings flapped erratically as they fell, their scaley armor penetrated by unforgiving rounds speeding at 1,800 miles per hour! I raised my fist as I released the trigger, turned and dove to evade the return belches of fire.

Chaos in the skies over the Black Forest! How it looked from the ground, should any farmer brave the sight of the dragons and the noisy contraptions fighting them, I shall never know and could only dimly contemplate. Our formation, such that it was, scattered to all compass points as we neared their breath range and fire erupted in vast gouts, oily smoke smearing the perfect blue dome.

My turning dive became too fast, too shallow, and I found my Fokker shuddering, the stick hardly having any effect, feeling mushy, on the verge of losing lift, which would have locked me in a stall-spin, a death-spiral. I leveled out to avoid catastrophe. Which was fortuitous, as a scaley maroon-black male with yellow eyes banked almost right in front of me, belly exposed.

I turned left, banking and hard, subjecting myself to extra earth gravities. I fired, the belt of bullets pumping through the barrels, shells falling behind and away to the forest below.

Blood erupted from my scoring and the dragon's wings spread to their full, intimidating span. He glided past me, blood wind-blown in dollops from thewounds riddling his chest, surely, hopefully, puncturing his heart and lungs. I looked behind, the neck of the beast no longer tensed as a spring but twisting in on itself in agony. Surely he would expire before he reached the earth.

"That was for Schneider!" I cried, delirious with the kill.

I scanned in all directions. Smoke, from dragonfire, from machine gun fire, from engine exhaust, interfered with visibility on this otherwise clear day. I could see a few of my comrades. And also, several dragons. Two above, one level to the west, my left. We passed one another and I made my turn with intent to come up behind her. I noted her two horns and not six, thus, a female with larger fire sacs. I hoped the excessive noise of our squadron had the beast I targeted unaware of my tracking maneuvers. For if she spotted me, I knew from experience she could spin around by the diameter of a coin and bathe me in flame. But the limitations of their fire sac may prove another advantage. No one in recorded history had ever witnessed a single dragon spitting fire more than five times across a day. Most could only manage two or three.

I turned, steady, multiple gravities pushing me as I throttled. My hopes soared as the tail of the beast, the fins at the end acting as a stabilizer like the tail of my aircraft, swung closer to my iron sight. The neck of that serpentine monster turned to the side with astonishing quickness, her finding an enemy approaching with fixed wings and a spinning propeller. I swear to my ancestors that we locked eyes for a fateful second, and despite the distance, did I see fury within?

And time, by my experience, slowed, as if someone held their finger on the minute hand of a clock, making the world dreamlike in sluggishness. The dragon's neck swung down, and their body followed. I tried to mimic the dive, forcing the stick down, ready to fire. The beast's wings flared wide, arresting their descent, slipping within in my sight and I fired, missing, as the maneuver continued, one wing folding. Her body spun, a damned ballet dancer of the very atmosphere, the tucked wing again spreading, then both wings flapped and she disappeared from my sight. It flew beneath and had risen behind me! I turned evasively, hard, to the right, hoping that I'd chosen the correct path to avoid the coming firestorm. I felt the heat blaze through my jacket, saw the orange glow upon my gloves, and my doom on the heels of that.

I looked up, wholly uncooked, cold air slipping through my woolen scarf once again. I checked my left wings, now blackened at the tips. Behind me, the dragon roared like a lion enraged. I suspected that was the final arrow of fire in her quiver this day, and she had missed her quarry.

I leveled out and moved the throttle ball to the firewall once again. The dragon still gave chase, but I was faster. I didn't have to fear those jaws that could remove my wings with little effort.

Looking back, my pursuer arched her neck up, then dove from my view in an instant. I maintained my course.

A fellow Fokker descended behind me, pursuing that dragon, guns blazing.

I grabbed my canteen and wetted my parched mouth, the metal cold on my lips. I extracted my pocket watch; it was near time to head back for fuel. My fuel indicator told of even less time remaining.

I scanned the sky all around, making short clearing turns for 360-degree visibility. Unless the air battle had gotten far too scattered, I could see far more planes than dragons. I counted sixteen Fokkers within sight. The other squadron, Emil's, had arrived!

I could return to base—the battle was won.

And dear Emil! I'll see you in an hour!

•　　　•　　　•

Dearest Elsabeth,

By the time this missive reaches you, you will have read of the great battle in the sky from the newspapers. Im Deutschen Reich declared in a headline, "Man's Technology Defeats Dragons in Sky War!" The headlines across Europe buoyed my heart, despite the deaths of several comrades. And a close friend, Lt. Emil Hahn, remains missing, but I'm keeping my hopes alive.

Uncertain if the newspapers are telling the whole story, I shall attempt to interpret for you these events and their meaning to Europe, and to the world at large. The peace treaty inked more than a millenia past, Foedus Pacis Inter Dracones et Homines, in short, where people would provide the dragons with stock for food and neither species would attack the other. And so we tended pastures of Great Oxen in Greece, elephants in Sicily, and so on. Our treaty with the Union of Claw, the formal name for the dragon nests of Western Europe, had been effectively nullified a century ago in 1821 when the Danes bombarded the nest in the Scandinavian Mountains, crushing many of the hibernating reptilian inhabitants. The retaliation came the following summer, the burning of Stockholm. Things quieted temporarily after that, but this tit-for-tat played out every decade or two, the latest occurring these weeks past.

The goal with our war footing: extermination, if possible, renegotiation to a more favorable treaty, if not. We shan't be forever food-farming slaves to these man-eating, vile creatures. It happened in the Americas. The Wabanaki Confederacy first developed flight, and employed their machines as a brokering leverage to force the dragon nests from their midst to the coasts, where the dragons re-learned their ancient art of whaling for food, and resolved to leave human affairs alone. Bless those inspirational people across the Atlantic!

I have gone on at length, perhaps boring you. Give Wilhelm my affection and tell him to stick to his studies!

With Love and Hope,
Johann

•   •   •

27 NOVEMBER 1916

Hospitals: dreary places of blood and foul odors. I sat next to heavily bandaged Emil in his bed. He slept, his consciousness mercifully dampened by morphine. I wanted to take his hand in mine, to whisper that everything would be fine in the coming weeks, to weather the wounds and the pain and the healing. But there I sat on a stiff wooden chair, hands folded, feeling as useless as a rudder with a snapped cable.

But I had to be near him. Knowing he had sustained terrible injuries tore my heart. My recent performance in the sky earned me the right to be at the bedside of my dearest friend. My commanding officer didn't hesitate in writing up my leave. But had I wrecked my Fokker instead of killing a dragon, everything would have been different, and Emil would have been alone. My heart could not have withstood such a trial.

Bandages covered his face, neck, and left arm. His plane had suffered a gout of dragonfire, but remained intact. I had been told the flames did not deteriorate the wings before he managed to ditch in a lake, where an elderly fisherman rowed to his smoking aircraft, afloat.

The wait agonized me. I drank coffee. I read newspapers. I smoked. I briefly left the hospital and procured two novels from the library. Hours had passed before Emil stirred from the morphine haze. I sat the library copy of *The Metamorphosis* on the floor (to never open it again, how hideous!) and took his hand in mine. "Emil?" I whispered.

Through that slit in the bandages his eye, the one not completely bandaged over and lost to the flames, fluttered, opened, and focused.

"Should I get the nurse?" I asked. "Do you need anything?"

His hand squeezed mine. As I patted the back of his hand, my heart cheered.

"Johann," he whispered, speech slurred. "You should leave."

"What? No! I'm not leaving your side, dear friend. Shall I get the nurse?"

"Leave me. Go to your wife. Find another friend."

Ah. The morphine talking, surely. Or the pain of his burns had returned and he saw Death behind me, scythe in a bony hand. "If I leave, it's to fetch a nurse."

"I saw myself in the water."

So, his mind was clear as a freshwater lake. I whispered in reply, "So your rugged handsome face got a touch more rugged. What kind of monster would I be if I left a dear friend in the time of his direst need? I cannot, Lieutenant, therefore I won't. Now. Would you like some water? You sound parched."

• • •

28 NOVEMBER 1916

I read the day's headlines to Emil. At first, I tried to find only positive articles and quickly realized those were so few. But I lead with, "Army Raid on Great Oxen Pasture Successful!" I continued with the drophead below: "Two Dragons Slain in Battle!"

"Nice," he rasped. I had learned that half of his left cheek and part of his lips had melted away. Talking for him was difficult. He spoke slowly and with a slur. "Next."

"Dragons from Southern Nests Spotted Migrating Toward Germania." Drophead: "Scale Spies Likely Spread Word of Our Military Successes."

"Foul people."

I shook my head. "Vermin."

"Next."

A nurse appeared in the doorway. "Lieutenant Fischer?"

"Yes?"

"Urgent phone call."

I folded the paper and patted Emil's shoulder. "Be right back." Down the hall at the desk waited the receiver on its side. I answered with rank and name.

My CO responded in kind. "Back to base. Immediately."

"Sir, if I may plead for another day—"

"This is a direct order, Lieutenant."

I stopped myself from protesting further.

"Don't think that I haven't heard the rumors of your morally questionable relationship with Hahn. If it weren't for your surprising skill and bravery in the air, you'd be in the brig awaiting trial. Attacks may be imminent. Your ... *friend* will recover without you."

•   •   •

23 DECEMBER 1916

After another defensive posture reconnaissance flight around Stuttgart, I drank tea watching the sky purple in the dusk as a corporal refueled my Fokker. An unseasonably warm day, and right before Christmas Eve. No white Christmas for us.

I planned to take the train into Stuttgart the next morning to spend it with Emil, still in a hospital bed, followed by dinner with Elsabeth and Wilhem. Emil had endured a successful skin graft surgery a week previous. His family had abandoned him as a teen, yet he'd used his father's military credentials to join the Army Air Service, just to spite him. He knew full well his father would never spill that family secret to his military comrades. Like myself, he was fascinated, obsessed even, with the new flying machines.

Someone came running from the hangar, arms flapping with great or terrible news. The private, puffing, exclaimed, "They're attacking! Stuttgart! Now!"

My heart stopped. I couldn't speak. Emil was there. And my family. And I was *not* there.

"Private, round up the squadron. With haste! Corporal, help him! I'll finish the refueling."

They exchanged a look and did not move.

"Now!" I roared. "That's an order!"

They ran.

I hopped up the stepladder and dispensed the fuel, which topped off in seconds. I spooled the hose back and looked at the line of planes. Three had been fueled. Nine had not.

The sky had darkened further.

Stuttgart was half an hour flight from the field. I could crank and fly my plane without the prechecks. I resolved to take that risk. I snatched the leather helmet and goggles from the prep table.

"Lieutenant!" barked the CO as he marched from the hangar.

I bound the helmet tight beneath my chin. I strapped on the goggles.

"You step on that ladder and you'll find yourself in the brig. Stand down! Now!"

I paused. I stood at attention and saluted. "A word, commander?"

"No." He stepped up to me, his handlebar moustache stiff as a rifle barrel, our noses almost touching.

"But Commander, my family—"

"No." He spoke level, the timbre of his voice was such that a thousand men would follow his orders without hesitation. "You're not the only man here with family in Stuttgart. You've lost your mind, Lieutenant. You might find your way to Stuttgart in the dark, but you wouldn't find your way back. And there, you wouldn't be able to target the beasts, but they could target you. They see better than us at night, the scientists say." He pointed at his eye, as if explaining to a toddler. "They've lived for thousands of generations in the sky, a life we've just begun to taste."

There was no argument to his logic, nor his command.

"Assembling your squadron for a suicide mission is unbecoming of a leader, Lieutenant Fischer. I knew you'd show your true face one day."

I stood silent. Waiting.

"We fight for all Germania. Not a single ... *man's* ... family." With that last line he eyed me with one eyebrow lifted. "The city is ringed with searchlights and mobile M1914 machine guns. Stuttgart was laid as a trap. We'll chop them up from the ground. Understand?"

"Yes, sir."

"You're confined to your barracks until morning."

•   •   •

24 DECEMBER 1916

My Christmas Day leave had been rescinded. With anger and fear boiling in my belly like a stew, I packed my duffle. The news from Stuttgart was dire, despite the ballyhooed defenses. Parts of the city still burned, I heard, painting the sky gray with the ashes of the dead. The hospital stood unscathed, but there was no news of the neighborhood where Elsabeth and Wilhelm lived. My squadron was scheduled for a noon reconnaissance.

I took my desertion seriously. My nation had deserted me the day I dropped from my mother. Why should I stay? How could I risk my life for a nation that would condemn me, and everyone like me, to hard labor, or worse, for the essential act of existence?

If it were reported I had departed the base gate with my duffle, military police would be on my heels. I hitched a ride from several mechanics in a horse cart headed to the town for some Christmas revelry. From there, the train to Stuttgart. I had escaped. But the trains weren't operating the full distance: two Stuttgart train stations had been destroyed.

I made it to the hospital just after the sun had set. The hospital overflowed, a chaotic crowd surrounded the building. Patients and the dead were laid out in the gardens. I figured that's where they had placed Emil, recovered enough to suffer a night or more outside in a medical tent.

First, I checked the posted lists of the dead and wounded in a hall filled with the wails of the grieving. Relief flooded me: My wife's and son's names were not listed.

"There you are," I greeted Emil, his face and left arm still bandaged, but less thoroughly. He sat up on his cot with some effort.

His right eye widened in surprise. "You came all this way?"

"A small visit before Christmastime with Elsabeth and Wilhelm. And I have a gift." I patted my leather flight jacket, where the gift was hidden.

•　　　•　　　•

26 DECEMBER 1916

From the nurse station in the outdoor area of the hospital I stole several rolls of bandages and a half-full bottle of antiseptic. It was easy. And the guilt gnawed at me.

Emil sat awake and waiting, as planned. I helped him stand and we shared a gentle embrace. I wished it tighter, but his wounds still pained him grievously. He walked beside me and we kept walking. Away from the hospital, down the road. Waiting was the horse and carriage I had stolen from a family that had perished in the attack. We traveled the roads east. We did not pause for sleep, but kept our eyes open for any pursuers.

When discovered missing, would the Army Air Service search for me? This had been calculated by Emil. I was a hero, and my desertion was a grave embarrassment and would be a blow to morale throughout the military at a time of war. And although my commanding officer would want me brought back and hanged, he would cover up my traitorous act. He might well declare me dead. That was our conclusion. I hoped Emil was right. If not, if we were cornered, in my jacket lay the last resort, my Luger Pistole 08. They only way I would die for this empire would be by my own hand.

We planned to ride to the train station at Pforzheim. Days of train travel would conclude in Lisbon. From there we planned to emigrate to the Wabanaki Confederacy across the ocean: such a welcoming and advanced people. Emil would receive more surgery there. Until then I would be his nurse.

And we would be free.

•   •   •

My dearest Elsabeth,

I have wept nights over this letter. If I appeared sad at our Christmas dinner, I apologize. But I shall cherish those moments the remainder of my life.

I am in agony, and I do not wish suffering upon you or Wilhelm. You have suspected, surely, over the years, about my nature. I shall never apologize for that. But I apologize for trying to fit in with a society that abhors me. I am sorry I had gotten you involved through marriage. I am sorry for Wilhelm, too, and will miss both of you terribly. It is better for you both this way, than me being court-martialed and sent to prison, and the reason dragged through social circles and newspapers.

I have arranged for a trustworthy accountant to handle our affairs until Wilhelm comes of age. His information is within this letter.

I would never propose that you leave your beloved family for a foreign land, departing forever with a man that can never love you as you deserve. It so pains me that I will miss seeing Wilhelm become a man. Give him my love every day. I encourage you to move to the countryside until the war is over.

I do love you, Elsabeth, love is the reason for my departure. I hope one day you will understand.

With Love, as ever, and Hope for a better future,
Johann

ABOUT THE AUTHOR

Brian D. Hinson abandoned an unfulfilling career to take up part-time work and visit 40-some countries in the backpacker fashion. He slowed life even further to settle in rural New Mexico with his wife and three pitbulls to write science fiction. Short story "Disposable Gabriel," in December 2023 Cast of Wonders, made Nerds of a Feather's recommendation list for the 2024 Hugo award. "Distance and Family and Death" is featured in *Amazing Stories' Best of 2024*. Other stories in *Pseudopod, Andromeda Spaceways, Cossmass Infinities, On Spec Magazine, Shoreline of Infinity*, and more. For more information, visit *www.briandhinson.com*.

YOU MIGHT ALSO ENJOY

GREY MOTHER MOUNTAIN

by Elyse Russell

When her village is destroyed, an elderly woman seeks help from the last remaining dragon to get revenge.

SMASH THE WORLD'S SHELL

by Daniel Fliederbaum

When a mysterious ring suddenly appears on reclusive teenager Ellen's bookshelf, she is granted the power to travel far away from everything she's ever known.

A WRECK OF DRAGONS

by Elaine Isaak

Teens and their giant robots search for a new home for mankind, but the planet they discover belongs to the dragons.

WAR MAGE

by L. A. Jacob

First Magus Brent Rogers has just been transferred to Afghanistan. His mission: to convince four dragons into doing what the Army tells them to do.

Available in digital and trade paperback editions from
Water Dragon Publishing
waterdragonpublishing.com